A DIFFERENT TUNE

STORY

BRUCE WITTY

ILLUSTRATIONS

RICHARD LAURENT

Once upon a time, in a land far away,
everyone looked alike
and did things the same way.

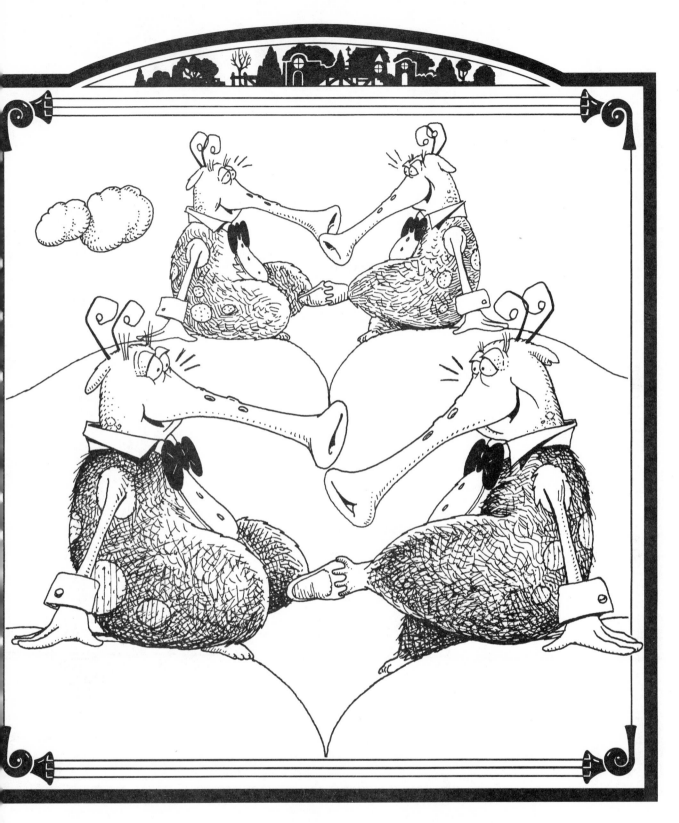

And everyone had the same thing to say.
"Hello. What's new? I'm fine. How are you?"

Each and every one played a tune on his nose.
They played the same tune
with their eight tiny toes.

Into this land, where all looked the same,
there came a stranger. Bill was his name.

Bill was different. It was easy to see.
Everyone thought Bill was the wrong way to be.

Bill's nose was short, not long like the rest.
Next to the others, Bill failed every test.

Bill had only six toes. The others had eight.
The others were early. Bill always was late.

Because he was different, Bill sometimes felt bad.
Bill tried to be happy but sometimes was sad.

To cheer himself up, Bill started to play
a tune on his nose in his own special way.

Bill used his fingers instead of his toes.
Bill used his fingers to tune up his nose.

Beautiful music Bill started to play.
The music was as sweet as a warm summer day.

The music made everyone open their ears.
It was music that everyone wanted to hear.

Yes, Bill was different from all of the rest.
Yes, Bill was different,
and his music was best.

Bill could not do what the others could.
So Bill did what he could
and made something good.

Draw a line from each word to what it names.

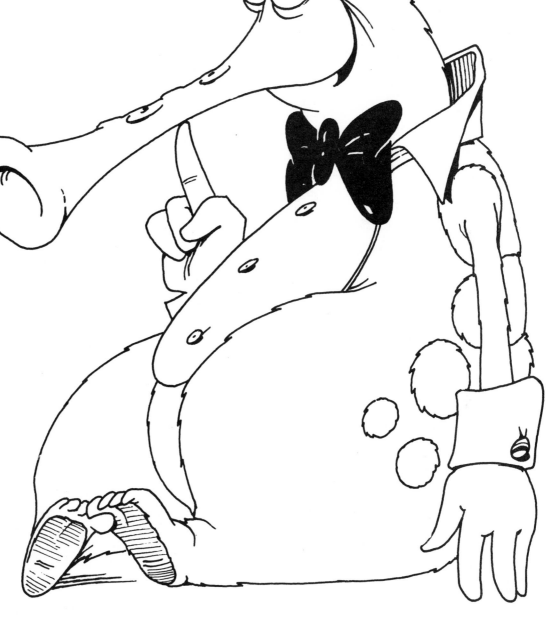

nose   **toes**   **fingers**   **ear**

Circle the word that goes with each picture.

happy   sad   old

early   late   new

old   sad   happy

new   late   early

Some words rhyme.
This means that they have the same last sound.
Bug rhymes with *rug.*
Pie rhymes with *sky.*
Draw a line between the words that rhyme.

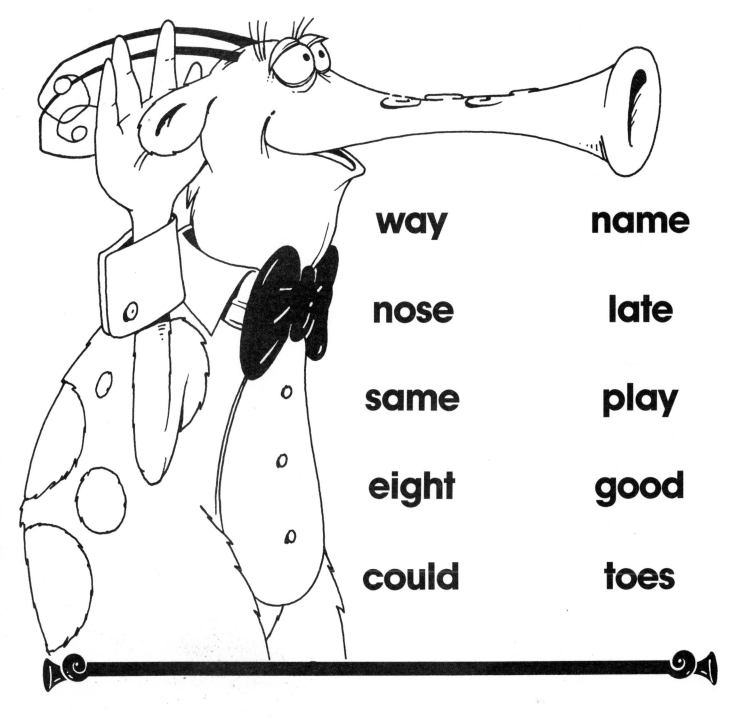

way	**name**
nose	**late**
same	**play**
eight	**good**
could	**toes**

Circle the correct word to answer each question.

What does Bill use to play a tune on his nose?

      toes   fingers   music

What does everyone else use?

      ears   fingers   toes

Who is the stranger?

      everyone   Bill   Betty

Who sometimes feels bad?

      Bill   Betty   Bob

Good is the opposite of *bad*.
Big is the opposite of *little*.
Draw a line from each word to its opposite.

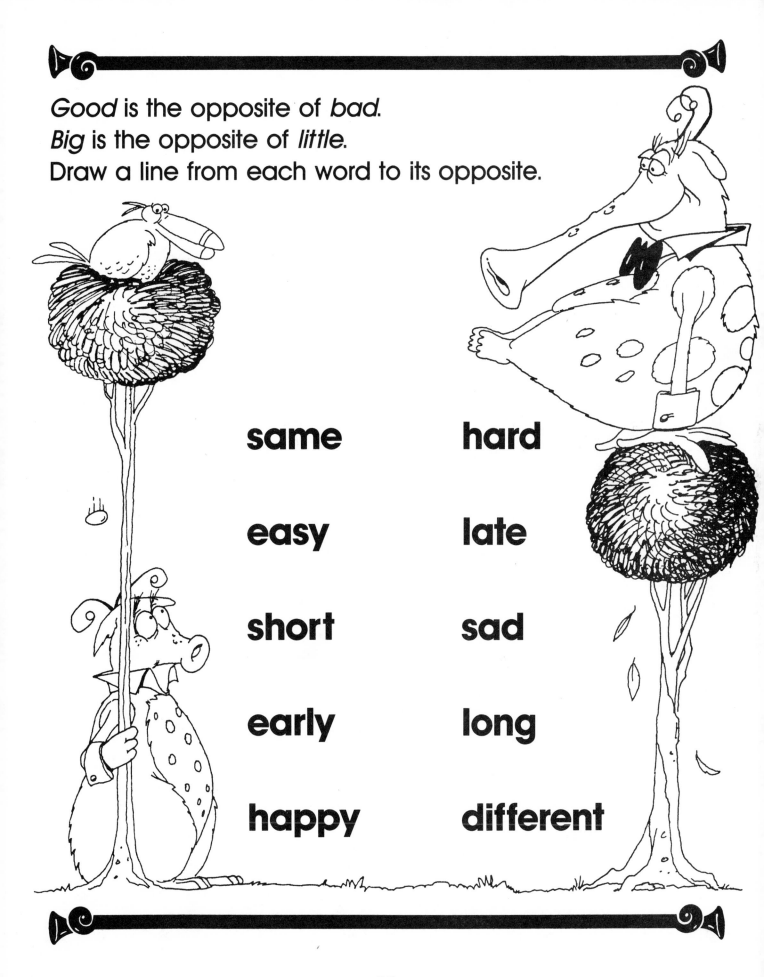

same   hard

easy   late

short   sad

early   long

happy   different

Read each question.
Circle the picture that answers each question.

Who looks alike?

Who has eight toes?

Who looks different?

Who has a short nose?

Read each of the four words.
Write each word where it belongs in the puzzle.

ears   music   fingers   different

ACROSS

1. Bill is _____ .

3. Bill's music makes everyone open their _____ .

4. Bill plays beautiful _____ .

DOWN

2. Bill used his _____ instead of his toes.

Read each sentence.
Circle **Yes** if it is true.
Circle **No** if it is not true.

Yes   No   Bill has eight toes.

Yes   No   Everyone else has eight toes.

Yes   No   Bill has a short nose.

Yes   No   Bill was sometimes sad.

Yes   No   Everyone likes Bill's music.

Read each sentence.
Write in the missing words.

The title of the story is

_____.

In the story, everyone looks the _____.

Then a stranger named _____ comes

into the land.

Bill plays a different tune on his _____.

Everyone _____ Bill's music.

Underline the correct answer to each question.

What does everyone say?

"Hello. What's new? I'm fine. How are you?"

"Hello. Don't go away. You're strange, I do say."

What does everyone think of Bill?

They think he is the right way to be.

They think he is the wrong way to be.

Why does Bill sometimes feel bad?

He feels bad because he is different.

He feels bad because he is late.

What kind of music does Bill play?

He plays loud music.

He plays beautiful music.

Read each question.
Circle the picture that answers each question.

Who is Bill's father?

Who is Bill's mother?

What can Bill do that everyone else can not do?

Write **1** by what happened first.
Write **2** by what happened next.
Write **3** by what happened after that.
Write **4** by what happened last.

_____ **Bill cheers himself up by playing a tune on his nose.**

_____ **Bill is a stranger who comes to the land.**

_____ **Everyone likes Bill's music.**

_____ **Everyone thinks Bill is the wrong way to be.**

28

Think about the story, *A Different Tune.*

What does it mean?

Read the two paragraphs below.

Circle the one that tells what the story means.

It is wrong to be different. You should try to be like everybody else. A person who is different can not do anything good. Nobody likes a person who is different.

It is not wrong to be different. It is not wrong to look different and do things in a different way. A person who is different can do some wonderful things. People who look the same can like somebody who looks different.

The title of the story is *A Different Tune.*
Sometimes there are many good titles for a story.
Read the titles below.
Three of them are good for this story.
Make an **X** next to the lines that are good for this story.

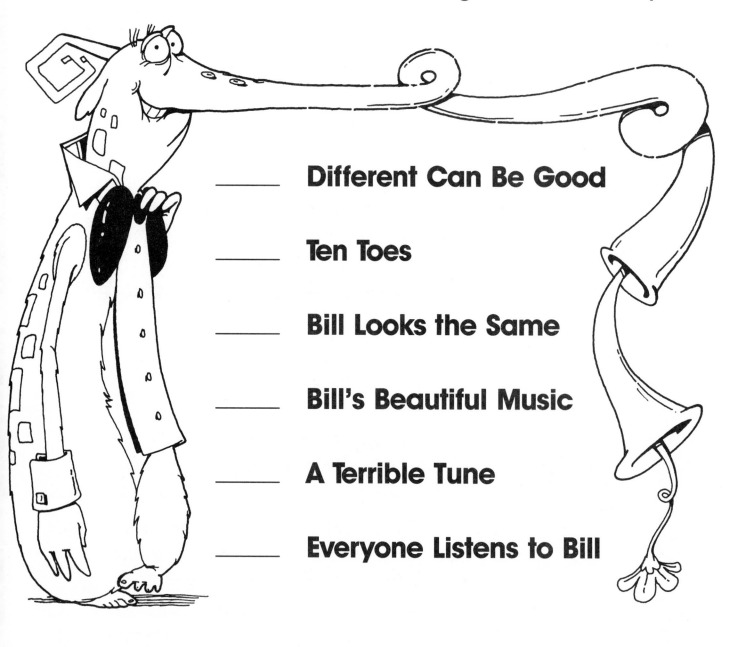

_____ **Different Can Be Good**

_____ **Ten Toes**

_____ **Bill Looks the Same**

_____ **Bill's Beautiful Music**

_____ **A Terrible Tune**

_____ **Everyone Listens to Bill**

Look at the last page of the story.
Think about the story.
Write about how Bill feels at the end.

_____

_____

_____

_____

_____

_____

THE
I CAN READ
AND
I CAN THINK
AWARD

Name _____

Title of Book _____

_____

02603